For Tim, Arthur, and Ada —S.S.

For Richard, always —S.M.

I Love You All Year Through

Stephanie Stansbie   ILLUSTRATED BY Suzie Mason

Random House   New York

I love you in the winter when the frost is on the trees.

When ice lights up the night
and snowflakes drift
upon the breeze.

I love you

when the snowfall

drips

and slowly
melts away.

And, waking up to spring,
we sit and welcome
a new day.

I love the blossom
blooming

as we **while away**

the hours.

Then joyfully
we splash about

through all the
April showers.

I love you when

the hazy summer

shimmers

all around.

And, lazy-warm, we curl up
side by side
upon the ground.

I love the **autumn**
turning leaves
from **green**
to **red** and **gold**.

And **knowing** that we'll **soon** be snuggled close against the cold.

In wind and rain and sun,
from **dawn** to **dusk**

and all year through...

You are my **darling**
precious one.
Forever
I'll love you!